The Littles
Get Lost

Adapted by **Teddy Slater**
from *The Littles And Their Amazing New Friend*
by **John Peterson**
Illustrated by **Jacqueline Rogers**

SCHOLASTIC INC.
New York Toronto London Auckland Sydney
Mexico City New Delhi Hong Kong Buenos Aires

The Littles are just
a few inches tall.
They all have nice,
long tails.

The Littles live
in the walls of the
Bigg family's house.

But don't tell that
to the Biggs. . . .
They have never seen the
tiny people.

One rainy day,

Tom and Lucy Little

went into Henry Bigg's room.

They wanted to find

something to read.

Henry was at school.

"I love this book,"
said Tom.
"I bet we could find
a tiny cave
in the woods!"

"But woods are a whole
block away," Lucy said.
"We could never walk that far
by ourselves."

The next day, Lucy
heard Henry Bigg
talking to his friend.
They were going to the
woods to have a picnic.
Lucy ran to tell Tom.

That afternoon,
Henry and his friend
packed a picnic basket.
Inside were blankets,
sandwiches, cold sodas —
and two tiny hitchhikers.

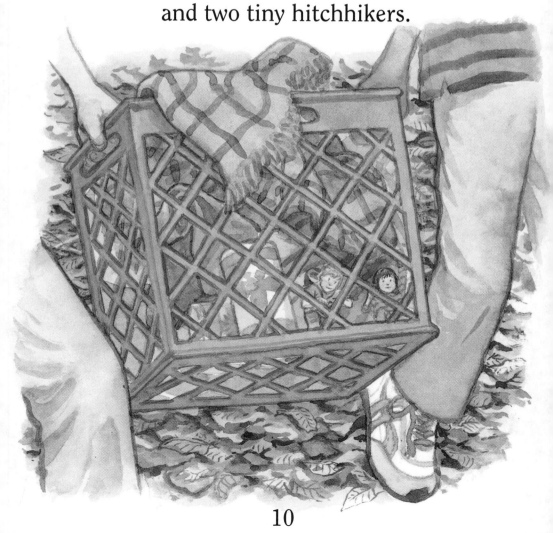

The boys went

across the Biggs' yard,

over the rock wall,

and into the woods.

They kept swinging the basket.

Tom and Lucy

were getting dizzy.

At last, the boys

put the basket down.

They ran off to pick wild

blueberries.

"Look for a hole in
the ground, Lucy," said Tom.
"It could be the back way
into a cave."

Suddenly, they heard
a loud sound above.
A dark shadow
covered the sun.
"Duck, Tom!" cried Lucy.

Tom and Lucy dropped to the
ground just in time.
A bee buzzed right over
them!

"Look, Tom!" Lucy cried.

"I think I found

our cave!"

"It's pitch-black
down there," Lucy said.
"That's why I brought
these candles," Tom said.

17

Lucy followed Tom

down,

down,

down

into the dark cave.

Soon, Tom and Lucy
came upon a small
room that was full
of seeds and nuts.

Then they passed
a room with a pile of
berries and mushrooms.
"I bet a wild animal
lives here," Lucy said.

"Don't worry," Tom said.
"Animals are afraid
of fire. Let's explore
the rest of the cave."

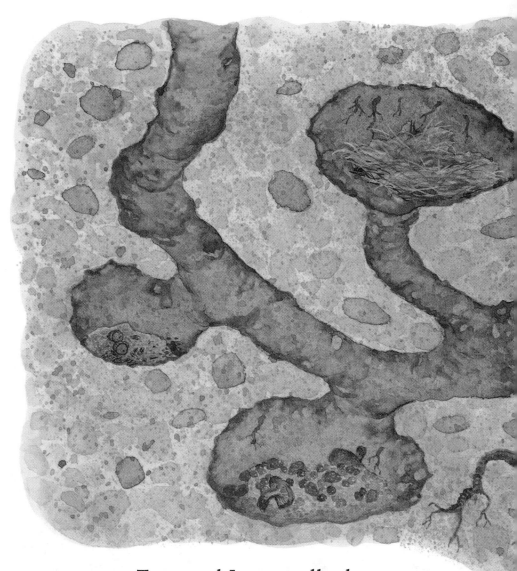

Tom and Lucy walked

around . . .

and around . . .

and around.

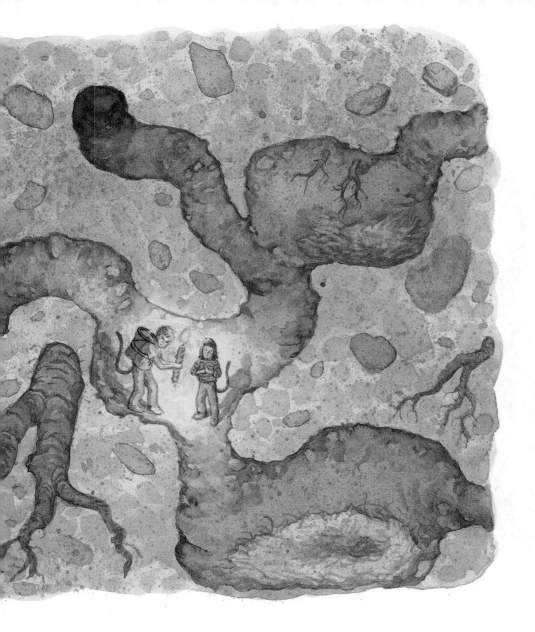

After a while Tom said,
"We'd better go back
before we get lost."

Just then, the candle

began to go out.

"Uh-oh," said Lucy.

"Don't move, Lucy," Tom said.
"I have another match here
somewhere."

By the time they could see again,

Tom and Lucy didn't know

which way to go.

"What do we do now?"

Lucy asked.

"Help!" cried Tom.

"HELP!" cried Lucy. "We're lost."

Swish!

Something moved in a
dim corner.

"What was that?" Lucy
whispered.

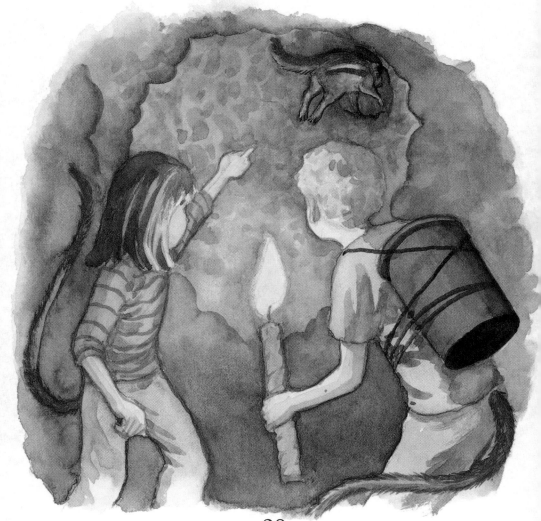

"It's a chipmunk,"
Tom said.
"That's who lives here!
And I bet she knows
the way out."

The chipmunk was moving fast.

Tom and Lucy had to

run to keep up.

The Littles followed

the chipmunk

into the bright, sunny day.

"Hooray!" they cried.

Back home, Lucy and
Tom had to agree:
It was fun going
into a cave—
but it was even more
fun coming out!